Your Friendly Neighborhood Spider-Man

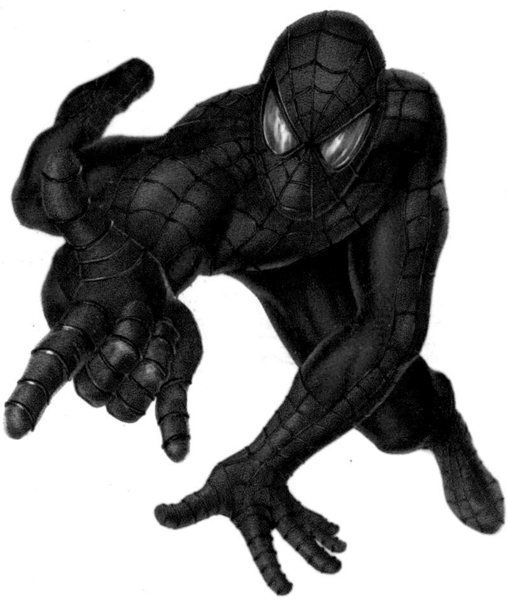

Written by Kitty Richards

Photography by Zade Rosenthal
and Steve Kahn

AVON BOOKS
An Imprint of HarperCollinsPublishers

SPIDER-MAN™

COLUMBIA PICTURES PRESENTS A MARVEL ENTERPRISES/LAURA ZISKIN PRODUCTION "SPIDER-MAN"
STARRING: TOBEY MAGUIRE WILLEM DAFOE KIRSTEN DUNST JAMES FRANCO CLIFF ROBERTSON ROSEMARY HARRIS MUSIC BY DANNY ELFMAN
EXECUTIVE PRODUCERS AVI ARAD STAN LEE SCREENPLAY BY DAVID KOEPP BASED ON THE MARVEL COMIC BOOK BY STAN LEE AND STEVE DITKO PRODUCED BY LAURA ZISKIN IAN BRYCE DIRECTED BY SAM RAIMI

MARVEL   PG-13   sony.com/Spider-Man   COLUMBIA PICTURES

Library of Congress Catalog Card Number: 2001118007
ISBN 0-06-442176-7

First Avon edition, 2002

AVON TRADEMARK REG. U.S. PAT. OFF. AND IN OTHER COUNTRIES,
MARCA REGISTRADA, HECHO EN U.S.A.

❖

Visit us on the World Wide Web!
www.harperchildrens.com
GO FOR THE ULTIMATE SPIN AT
www.sony.com/Spider-Man

PROLOGUE

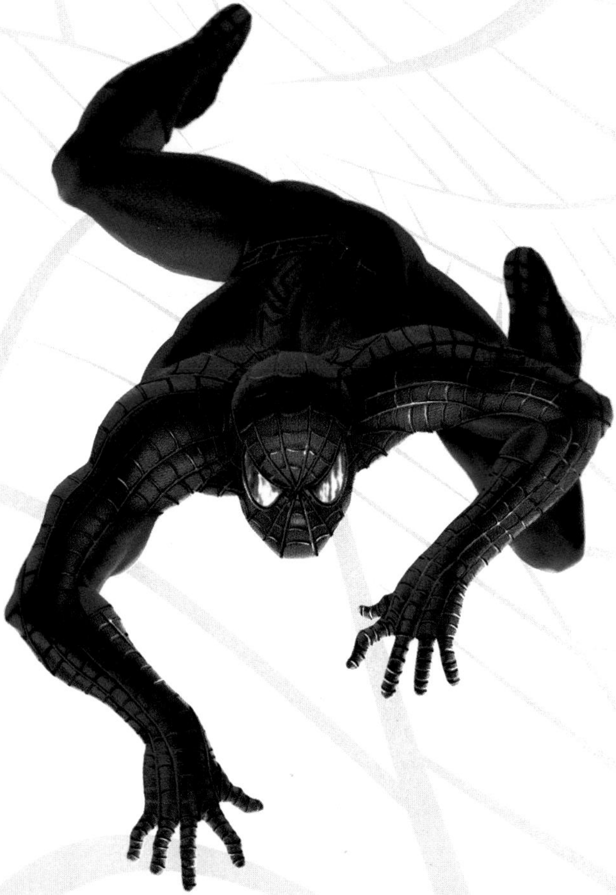

SPIDER-MAN

HOW IT ALL STARTED

Though Peter Parker definitely looked like an ordinary guy, he was anything but that. You see, back when he was a high-school student on a class trip to a laboratory at Columbia University, he had been bit by a genetically altered spider.

That's when his life changed. When he got home that evening, Peter passed out on the floor of his bedroom as a wimpy high-school senior in glasses. He woke up the very next morning with 20/20 vision, feeling stronger than ever. And that's not all—he suddenly possessed super spider-powers.

That's right. Peter Parker was a human spider.

Once Peter got his spider-powers under control and made himself a proper costume he became a bona fide superhero, catching petty thieves, defeating villains bent on world domination—you know the drill. But of course, superheroes don't get paychecks, and Peter had to do something to pay the rent. So he got a job as a freelance photographer. (Photography had always been an interest of his back in high school.) Taking pictures of what, you may ask? Peter was smart enough to realize that the world wanted pictures of Spider-Man, and who had better access to the web-slinger than Peter himself? By rigging a special timer to his camera he was able to provide the *Daily Bugle* with exclusive photos of the man in red and blue.

Being both a superhero crime fighter and a photographic journalist for one of the city's biggest newspapers, Peter became a very busy young man. Here are just a few adventures of your friendly neighborhood Spider-Man!

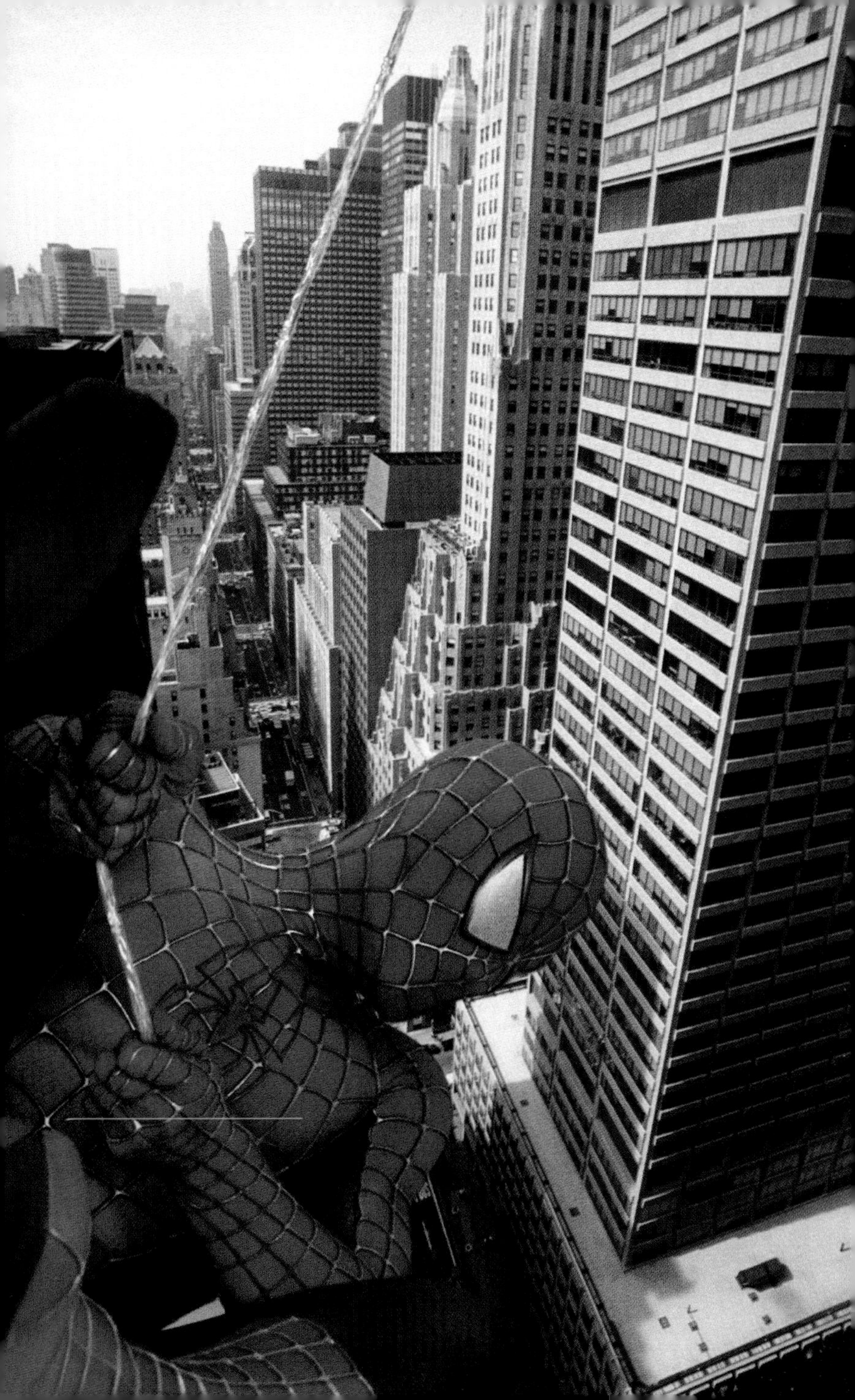

CHAPTER 1

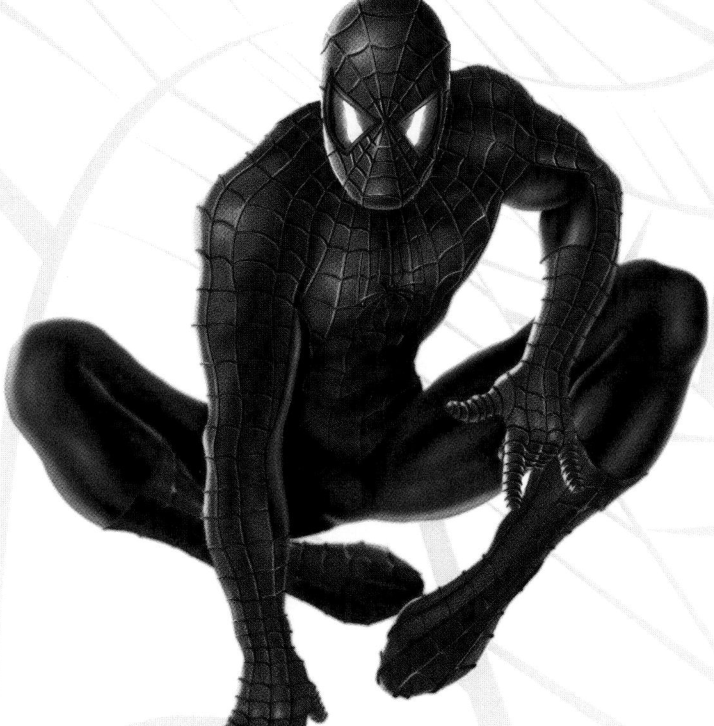

SPIDER-MAN

BATTER UP!

Peter Parker sat on the 7 train to Shea Stadium with butterflies in his stomach. After months of taking nothing but Spider-Man photos, he finally had an assignment he could really sink his teeth into—covering the New York Mets! Being a New Yorker from Queens, Peter had been to Shea Stadium many times and was really excited to actually sit in a field level seat (as opposed to the nosebleed seats he could afford in high school) and get up close to the action. He was kind of nervous because he had never covered a sporting event for the paper before, but he was ready to take on the challenge.

* * *

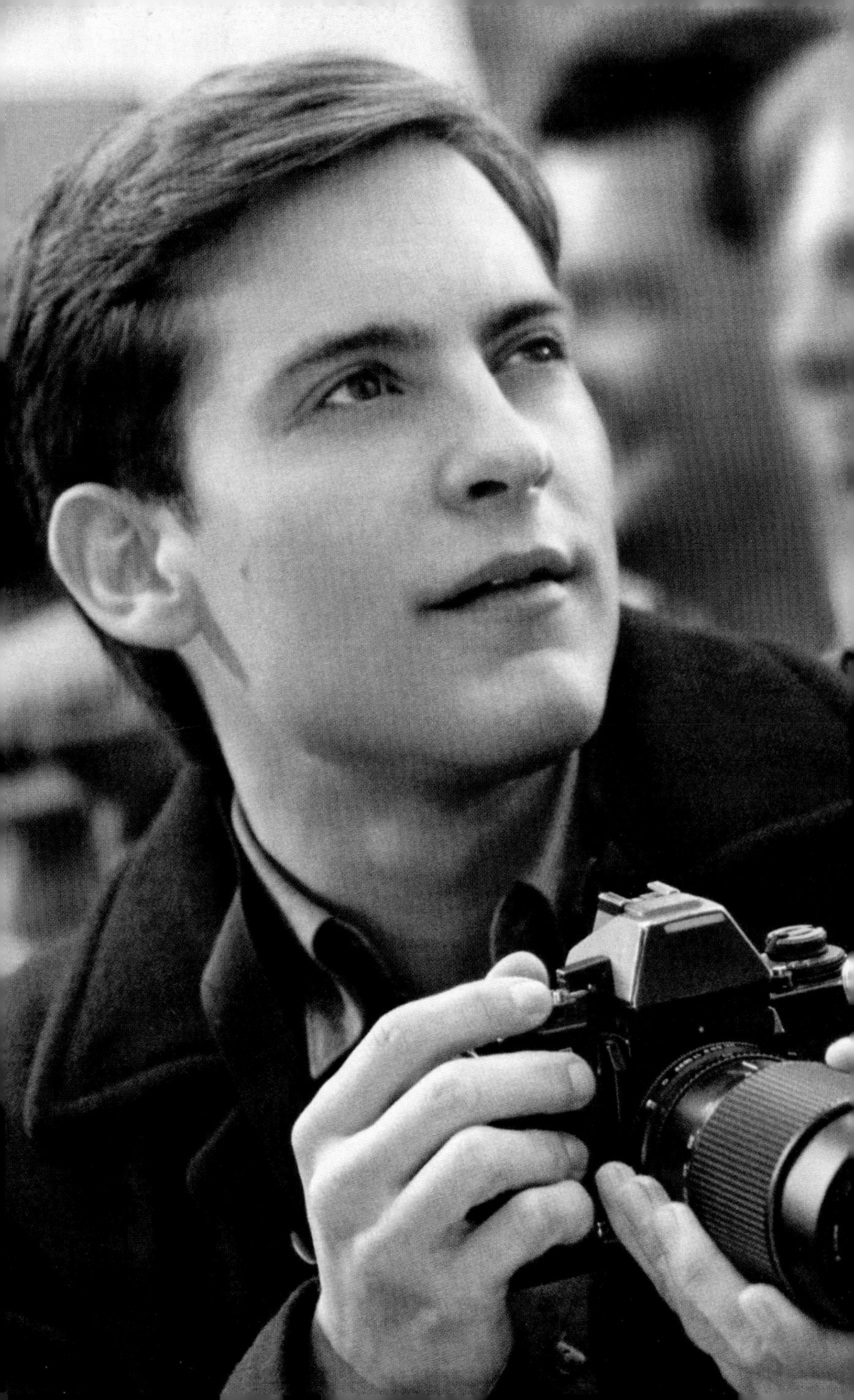

Peter was working on his third hot dog. He had taken dozens of great shots, including one of a diving play in the outfield. *Mr. Jameson is going to be really happy with me,* he thought. *Maybe I'll even get a promotion!*

Suddenly Peter started feeling weird—a little lightheaded. His spider sense was kicking in; something was about to happen. He could feel it. Peter stood up and ran into the men's room. He tore off his clothes to reveal his spider suit underneath.

When Spider-Man emerged from the bathroom, three police officers were running by. "We're after a jewel thief!" one of them shouted. "He's got a million dollars' worth of jewels in his bag! We had a car chase all the way from Manhattan!"

Spider-Man reentered the stadium, standing in the shadows to avoid being spotted by the crowd. But where was the thief? The stadium was packed—there was no way he or the cops would be able to spot him in this huge crowd.

That's when his spider sense kicked in

again. He glanced up at the screen in the out-field and saw that the cameras were trained on a very suspicious-looking guy running through the stands. Spider-Man pointed to the screen and the officer nodded excitedly. It was the jewel thief! And he was headed for an exit! How would they get to him in time? He was on the opposite side of the stadium, all the way by left field!

Spider-Man quickly shot a web into the stands on the other side of the arena. He flipped into the air, soaring high above the crowd. Twisting in the air, he did a perfect somer-sault and landed right in front of the thief. The crowd, no longer watching the game, roared their approval.

Spider-Man was just about to grab the thief when an unexpected thing happened.

In a panic, the thief ran straight down to the seats at field level, with Spider-Man right behind him. Then he dove over the rail-ing and ran onto the field! The crowd went wild! Players started chasing him, but no one could catch the thief. He was headed up the third-base line when Spider-Man swung onto the field. Just as the thief was about to cross home plate, Spider-Man zapped him with an extra-sticky line of webbing. The thief tripped and slid in the dirt. His bag opened and millions of dollars' worth of gems—diamonds, rubies, emeralds, and more—spilled across home plate.

"You're out!" said Spider-Man.

New York's Favorite Newspaper Since 1932

DAILY BUGLE

www.dailybugle.com 50¢

TAKE SPIDER-MAN OUT TO THE BALL GAME!

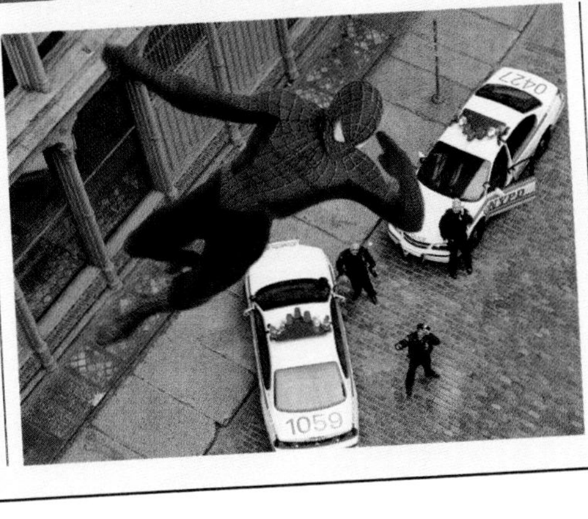
0427
NYPD
1059

By Tony Targo.

One, two, three strikes . . . Another criminal is out, thanks to Spider-Man! During the fifth inning of a Mets game last night, police chased a jewelry thief all the way into Shea Stadium. The thief had managed to get lost in the crowd when Spider-Man spotted him

(continued on page 2)

CHAPTER 2

A TOUGH ASSIGNMENT

"I just don't understand it!" J. Jonah Jameson yelled at Peter, who sat uncomfortably in a hard wooden chair in his boss's office. "You are the top Spider-Man photographer in New York City and you miss the shot of the century—Spider-Man chasing a thief on the infield at Shea Stadium! For the first time ever, we got scooped on Spider-Man by every other newspaper in town! We had to run a stock photo!"

Peter gulped. Though he had set up his special camera just in case, the stadium had been too big and he had missed all shots of the action. But in the excitement he had forgotten how disappointed his boss would be.

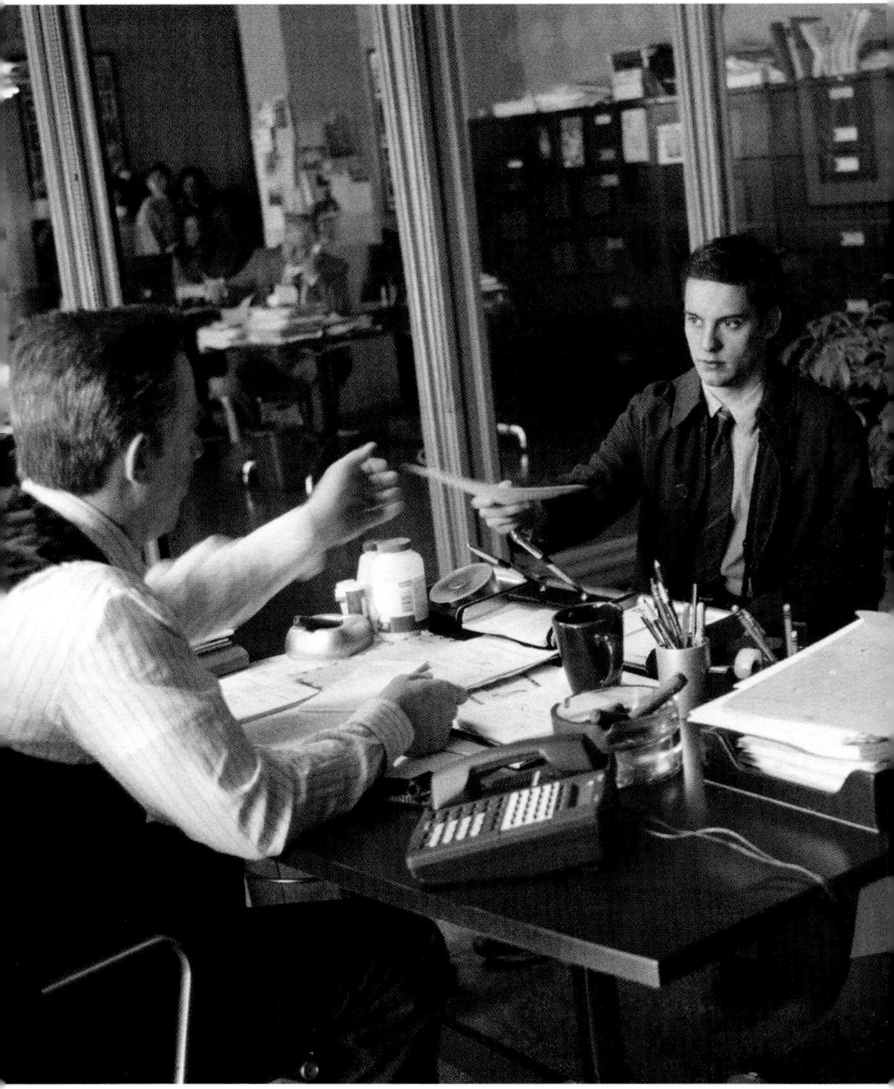

Maybe disappointed wasn't the word. Furious was more like it.

You didn't want to make J. Jonah Jameson furious, that was for sure. Especially if you wanted to keep your job.

"I promise I'll get a great shot of Spider-Man today!" Peter said.

J. Jonah narrowed his eyes at Peter. "You'd better, or you're fired!"

So much for that promotion, Peter thought. He would rig up his camera as usual, but what if nothing happened? This was not looking good.

Peter had just set up his camera on a nearby rooftop and was wondering what to do next when he heard a scream. Quickly he ducked into an alley and changed into his Spider-Man costume. Then he shot a web onto a nearby building and swung toward the voice.

When he arrived at the scene, an anxious crowd had gathered and was staring up at the side of a building. Peter craned his neck to see what was going on. It didn't look good. A window washer was dangling from his platform. A rope had snapped and so had his safety harness. Spider-Man began to scale the wall when he heard another *snap*!

"He's about to fall!" a woman shouted. "He can't hang on any longer! Spider-Man, help him!"

Thinking fast, Spider-Man jumped to the ground.

"What are you doing?" a man yelled. "Get up there!"

But Spider-Man knew there was no time. The man would fall in seconds. There wasn't a moment to lose!

Spider-Man began to work so fast that he was a blur to the crowd that watched in disbelief. Within seconds, at the base of the building, he had spun the biggest spiderweb the world had ever seen. And none too soon. For just as he finished the last strand, the man plummeted down—and landed safely in the strong webbing. He bounced once, twice, then came to rest, giving everyone on the ground a big thumbs-up! Spider-Man jumped up to release the man from the net and set him carefully on the ground.

The crowd cheered their approval. Spider-Man had once again bravely saved someone's life (and Peter's job)!

New York's Favorite Newspaper Since 1932

DAILY BUGLE

www.dailybugle.com 50¢

WEB-MASTER!

By Buck Decker.

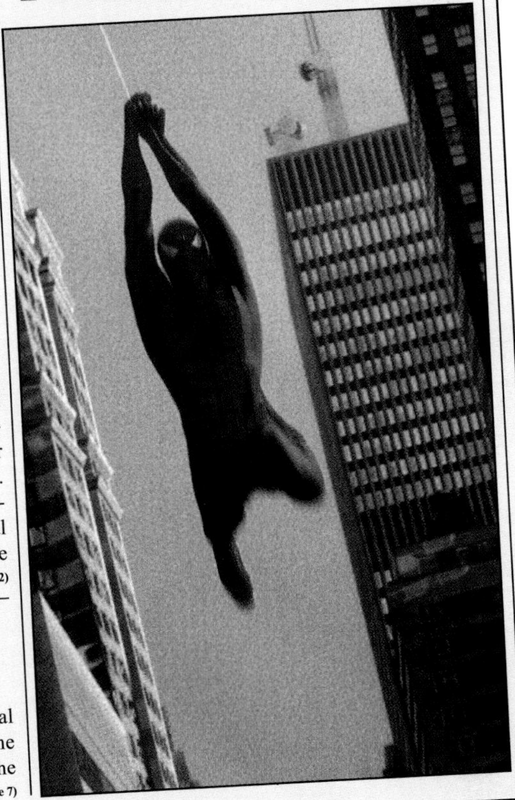

Does the Webslinger ever take a day off? Thankfully for the citizens of New York City, the word "vacation" is apparently not in Spider-Man's vocabulary.

Today, as a window washer was plummeting to most certain death, Spider-Man saved him by instantaneously creating a huge spiderweb to catch his fall. The forty-two-year-old father of four emerged without a scratch. "I owe my life to Spider-Man," said the grateful Brooklyn native as he

(continued on page 2)

City Plans New Policy

After months of legal wrangling between the Mayor's office and the

(continued on page 7)

CHAPTER 3

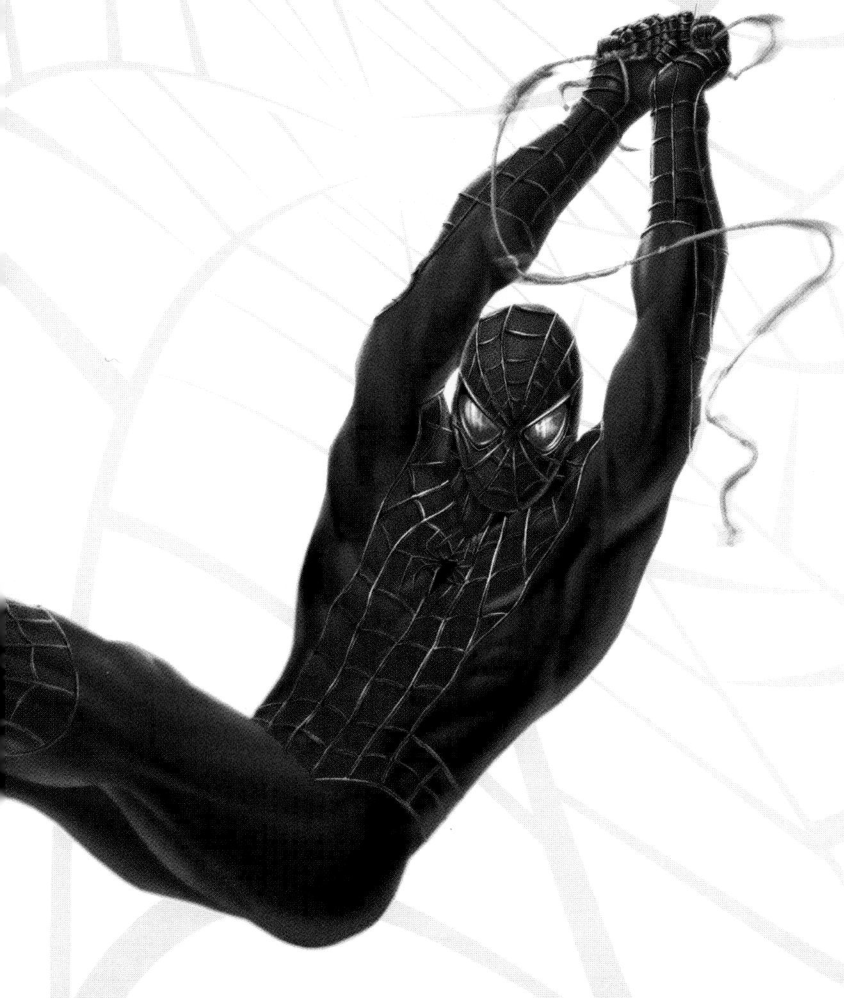

PETER'S DAY OFF

Peter woke up and smiled. It was his first day off in weeks. He was planning to take it easy—maybe watch a little TV, read a book, call some friends, or catch a movie. Even superheroes need to relax once in a while!

Peter had just popped two pieces of bread into the toaster and poured himself a glass of OJ when Aunt May called. She reminded him that he needed to go to the bank.

"Oh no. I forgot to deposit my paycheck!" he moaned. Peter knew his rent check, which he had written two days ago, would bounce if he didn't get to the bank as soon as possible.

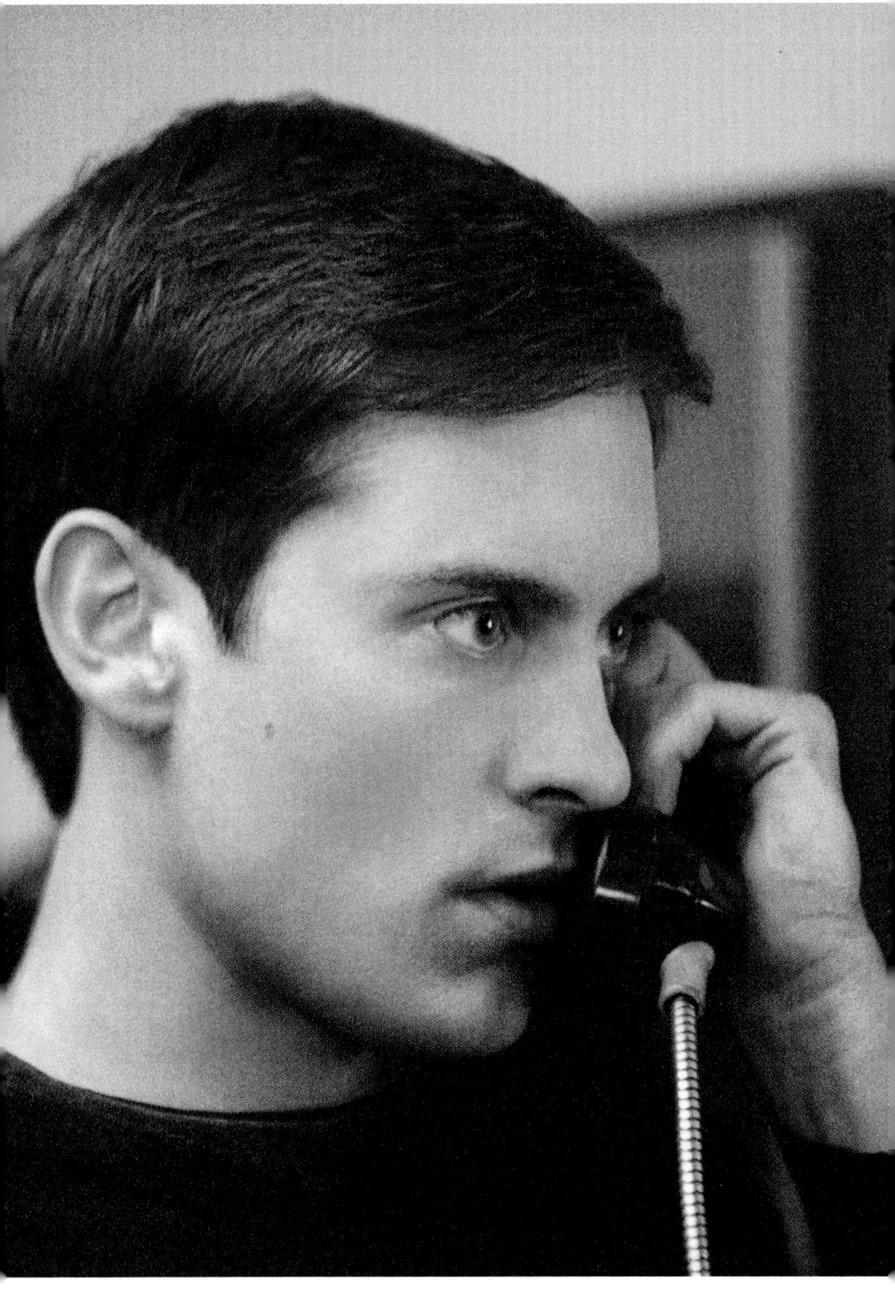

Peter sighed. "There goes my leisurely morning."

The line at the bank was long. With a shrug, Peter joined the end of it, opened up his newspaper, and began reading. He was scanning the comics page when he got that feeling again: the tingling spider sense that told him that he—or someone nearby—was in danger. It was very, very strong this time. Peter slipped off the line and ducked behind a pillar to strip down to his Spider-Man costume.

"This is a holdup!" a voice boomed. "Everyone down on the floor. If you follow my directions, no one will get hurt!"

Spider-Man peered around the pillar. There were three robbers in black knit caps. Two of them had guns. The other one had a big bag that he apparently was planning to fill with lots of money from the bank! The robber with the bag walked up to a teller's window and the other two stayed behind to keep their eyes—and their guns—trained on the bank customers, who were all lying facedown on the floor. "Nobody make a move!" they warned.

And nobody moved a muscle—except for Spider-Man. But he knew he had to be extremely careful in a situation like this. One false move and a jittery bank robber could injure an innocent person.

Very quietly, he crept up the pillar toward the ceiling. He sat up there waiting patiently, like a spider waits for a fly to land in its web. He waited until one of the gun-toting bank robbers turned his head. And in that split second, Spider-Man lowered himself halfway down from the ceiling on a web. Putting one hand over the robber's mouth, he quickly spun the man around and around, covering him with a thick coating of spiderwebbing, like an insect about become a spider's next meal! Then he pulled the robber up to the ceiling and fastened him there. He was wrapped up so tightly he couldn't move.

All of this was done so quickly that the second gunman didn't even notice anything was wrong until he turned around and couldn't find his partner. "Hey, where did he go?" he

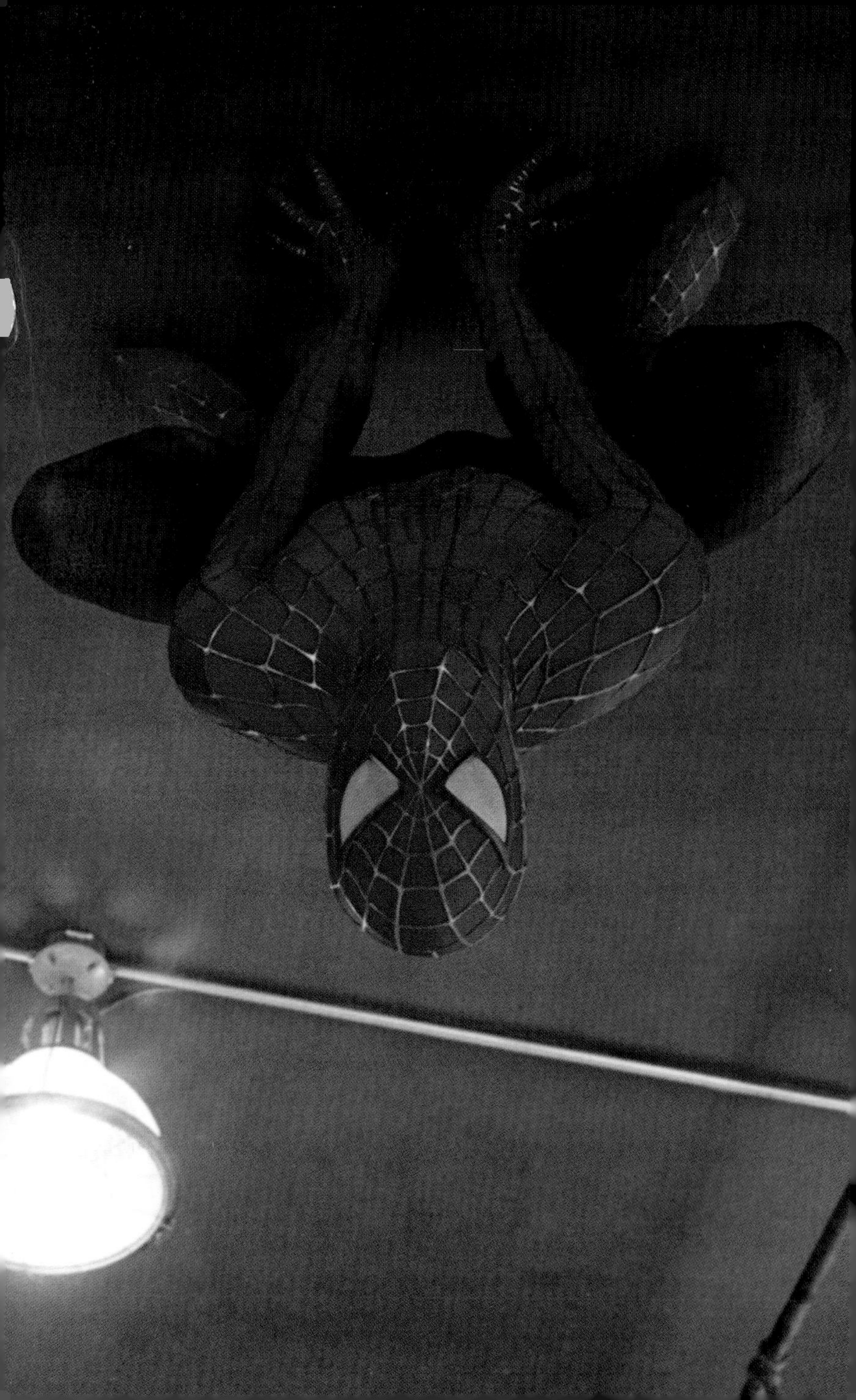

asked, dumbfounded. As he was looking around in confusion, Spider-Man secured him the very same way! Soon both of them were suspended from the ceiling—two of the biggest flies anyone had ever seen!

There! Now that the guns were out of the way, Spider-Man was ready for some more action. The other thief was stuffing his bag full of cash when Spider-Man lowered himself down from the ceiling, coming to a stop right behind him. Spider-Man tapped the robber on the shoulder.

"What?" the man said irritably. "Can't you see I'm busy?" He turned around and his mouth fell open. The robber looked around for his friends, but they were gone. In a panic, he started to run. The robber ran into the stairwell and headed straight up to the roof. But Spider-Man already knew where he was going, and got there first.

"You should really consider finding another career," said Spider-Man as the robber emerged from the stairwell.

Suddenly the robber charged at Spider-Man.

He pulled back his fist, about to punch Spider-Man right in the jaw. Of course, Spider-Man saw the whole thing coming and quickly stepped out of the way.

The robber flew past Spider-Man and tumbled off the roof. Spider-Man jumped after him. On the way down, he grabbed hold of the robber's coat and helped him safely to the ground.

When they reached the sidewalk everyone was shouting, "Hooray for Spider-Man!" Spider-Man smiled with the satisfaction of a job well done. But unfortunately, since the bank closed before Peter was able to make his deposit, his rent check bounced.

Poor Peter!

New York's Favorite Newspaper Since 1932

DAILY BUGLE

www.dailybugle.com 50¢

BANK HOLIDAY

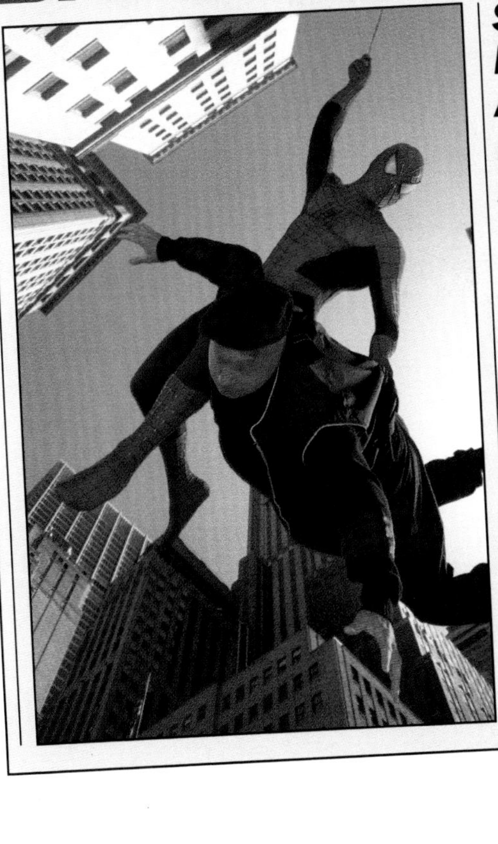

Spider-Man Foils Armed Robbery Attempt

By Tony Targo.

"It was horrible! Three men came in and held up the bank! Thank goodness that Centipede Man fellow was there to save the day!" said Mabel Saxon, age 82.

Sorry, Grandma, that's Spider-Man. But whatever you call him, New York City's favorite superhero was there once again to stop the city's worst criminals in their tracks.

(continued on page 2)

CHAPTER 4

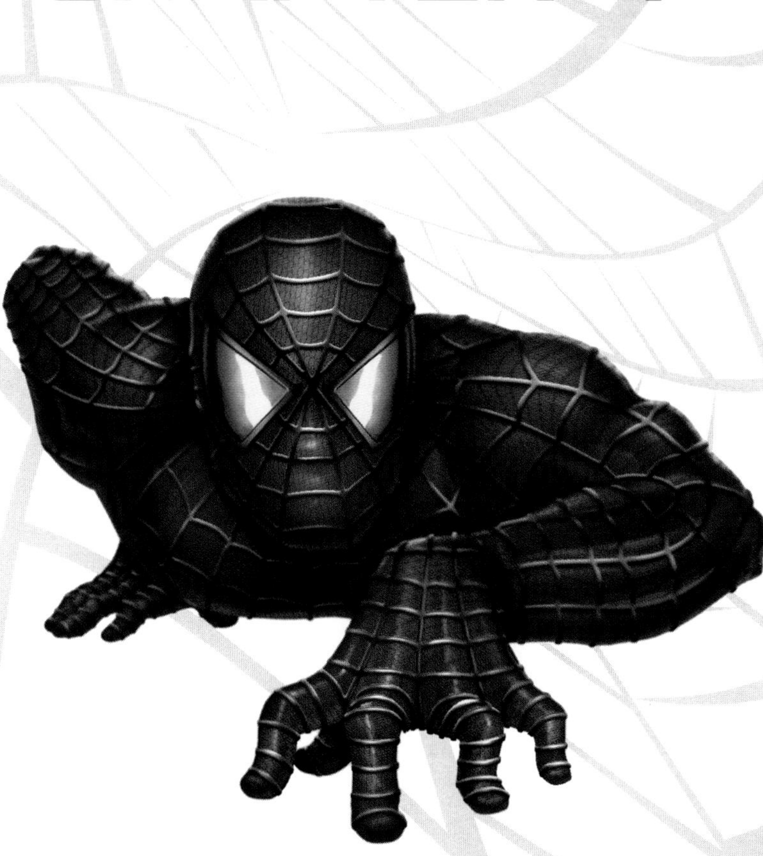

SPIDER-MAN

IT'S NOT FAIR!

"This was such a wonderful idea, Peter!"
said Aunt May.

It was a sunny weekend afternoon and
Peter and his aunt May had taken a trip outside the city to attend a real old-fashioned
county fair. There were livestock judging and
pie-eating contests and hayrides. But what
Aunt May loved best was the midway—with
the games, and the rides, and the food. They
ate corn dogs, candy apples, and cotton
candy until they were stuffed.

"I haven't had this much fun since I was a
girl!" said Aunt May. Peter looked over at his
aunt. Her cheeks were rosy and she had a
huge smile on her face.

Aunt May's favorite ride of all was the Ferris wheel. The two were waiting in line for their third time around when Peter's spider sense kicked in. Something was up!

"Sorry, Aunt May, but I think I'm going to sit this one out," he said. "Too much cotton candy, I guess."

"Okay, Peter. But you don't know what you're missing!" said Aunt May.

Peter scanned the crowd. What could be wrong? Everyone seemed to be having a great time, laughing and smiling and enjoying the fair. Just then, he heard it.

"Help! Help! My little girl!"

The fair-goers were pointing up to the sky. A hot-air balloon was floating above their heads. It appeared that no one was in it. Spider-Man looked closely. He could see a little hand on the basket edge!

"My little girl is in the balloon! Somebody save her!"

The crowd looked at one another in a panic. How could they possibly stop the balloon?

Peter ducked behind a game booth and stripped down to his Spider-Man costume. Then he ran out into the crowd and stared at the hot-air balloon. What was the safest way to stop the balloon? He could create a huge net above it, but it was windy, and he couldn't be sure which way the balloon would float. Or he could swing himself up to the basket and hope he could steer it to safety. . . .

"Oh no! It's headed toward the power lines!" someone shouted.

There was no more time to think. Spider-Man quickly raised his wrist and *splat*—he shot a line of webbing right at the bottom of the balloon's basket. It looked like Spider-Man was holding the string to the world's largest helium balloon! He was all set to start reeling it in when a huge gust of wind lifted the balloon higher in the air, pulling Spider-Man right up with it! The crowd gasped. Were Spider-Man and the little girl doomed?

Luckily, Spider-Man flew right by the Ferris wheel! He managed to grab onto it as he passed. Still clutching the web tightly in his hand, he clambered up the spokes of the wheel and sat in the seat right next to his aunt May!

"Oh, my!" she said.

After attaching the end of the web to the Ferris wheel bar with some extra-strong spiderwebbing, he carefully climbed up the web. He peeked over the edge of the basket to find a very scared little girl.

"Hi, Spider-Man," she whispered.

"Hi there," replied her rescuer. "You are going to have to wrap your arms around me very tightly and hold on. We're going to get you out of this balloon, okay?"

"Okay," replied the little girl. And she stretched out her tiny arms toward Spider-Man.

Next, Spider-Man reached in the basket and the child threw her arms around his neck. The two descended slowly to safety.

When they got to the ground he handed the girl over to her very grateful mother.

"Thank you, Spider-Man," she said, tears in her eyes. "You rescued my little one!"

Peter found his clothes, and returned to

39

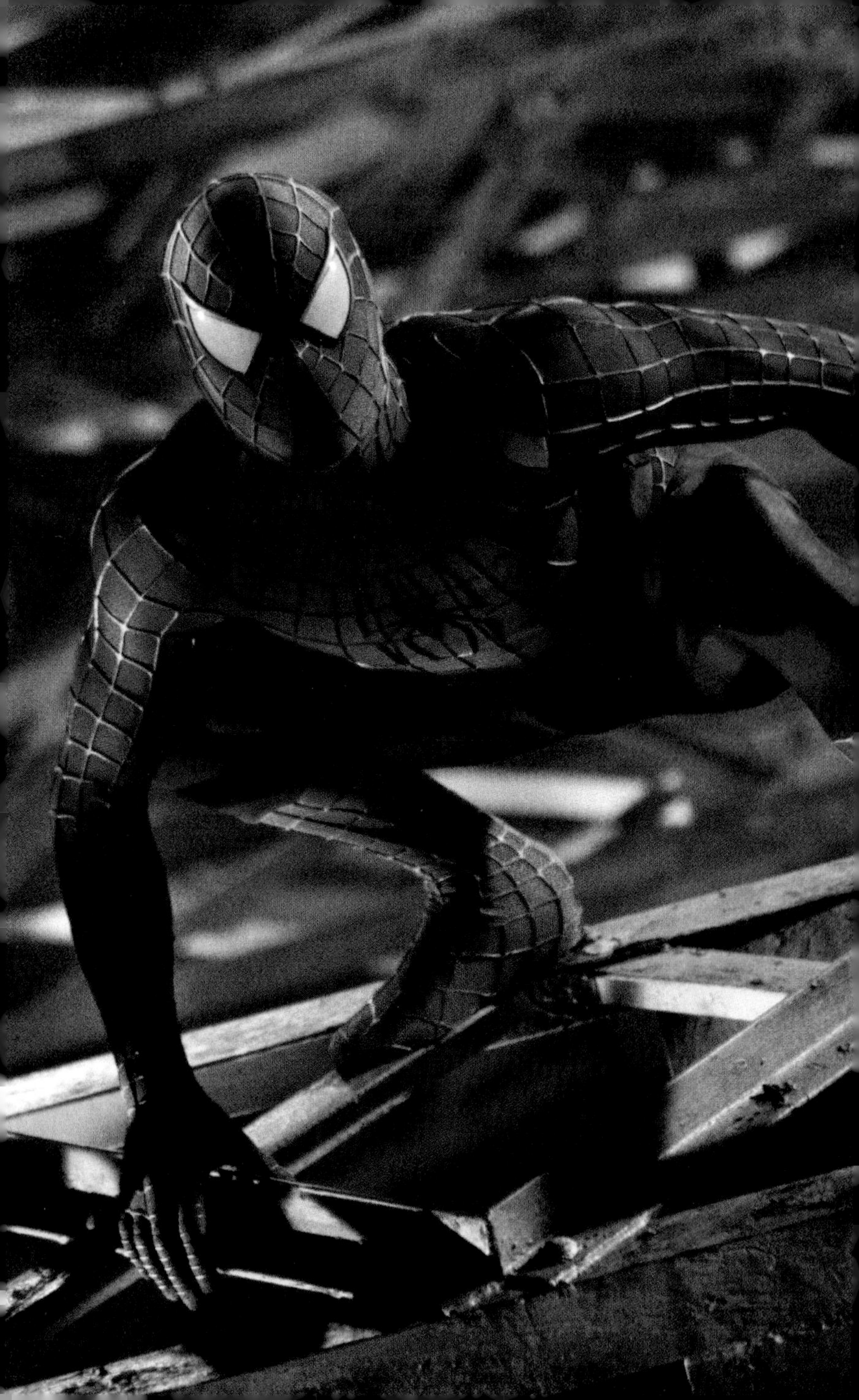

his aunt May, who was just getting off the Ferris wheel. "Peter! Peter!" she called. "Did you see it?"

"See what?" he asked.

"I can't believe you missed the excite-ment!" Aunt May gushed. "A little girl was in a runaway hot-air balloon, and guess who came to save her? He sat right next to me on the Ferris wheel!"

Peter pretended to think. "I can't guess. Tell me," he said.

"Spider-Man!" she said. "Just imagine, he was here at the fair today, too. What a coinci-dence!"

"What a coincidence," Peter repeated. "More cotton candy, Aunt May?"

"Don't mind if I do," she replied. "Make mine blue this time, please!"

Before Peter went for more cotton candy, he stopped to retrieve his camera. As usual, Peter had set up his camera just in case Spider-Man would have to spring into action. He didn't want to miss any more exclusive photos of the webslinger. He had gotten into enough trouble with Mr. Jameson the last time that happened.

Today he was sure he'd gotten great pictures of Spider-Man. Mr. Jameson would be happy. Maybe he would finally get a raise.

New York's Favorite Newspaper Since 1932

DAILY BUGLE

www.dailybugle.com 50¢

SPIDER-MAN'S FULL OF HOT AIR!

By Nancy Henson.

"She was headed for some power lines," said Fred Chambers, age 64, shaking his head in disbelief as he described watching a runaway hot-air balloon at the Wilmington County Fair today. "I thought the little girl in the basket was a goner. Then along came Spider-Man to save the day!" Chambers was one of hundreds of people who witnessed Spider-Man make yet another fantastic save

(continued on page 2)

CHAPTER 5

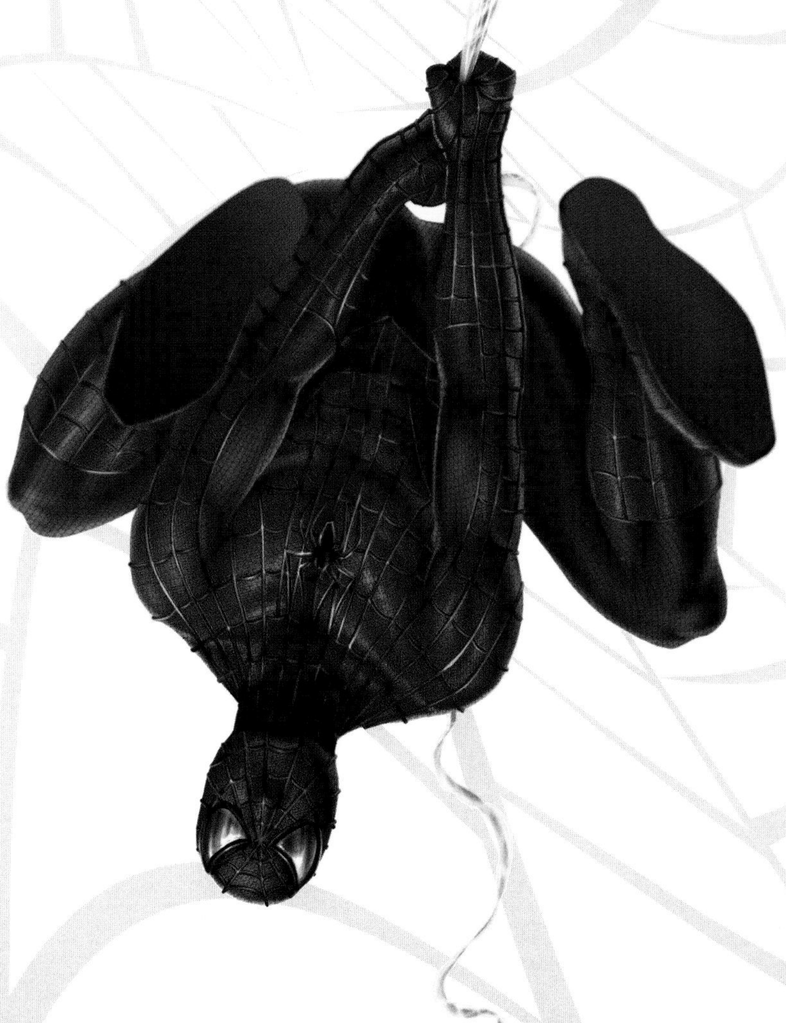

WHERE THERE'S SMOKE . . .

Peter was sitting on a city bus on his way to work. He was lost in a daydream about winning the Pulitzer prize for his photographs of something *other* than Spider-Man, when the blare of honking horns snapped him out of it. He realized that the traffic light had changed several times and they still hadn't moved. Traffic was at a standstill.

He walked to the front of the bus. "What's going on?" he asked the bus driver.

"Not sure," the driver replied. "But it's got to be something bad. They're redirecting traffic to Fifth Avenue and . . ."

Suddenly Peter's spider sense started up. "This stop please," he managed to say. He stumbled off the bus, but which way should he go? He looked up when suddenly he saw it—thick black smoke. Peter took off, running as fast as he could. He ducked into an alley and swung back out as Spider-Man. Then he made his way down the street as fast as he could.

When he got to the burning building, he could see the firefighters leading people out. Everyone appeared to be safe and sound. But then why was his spider sense still tingling?

Spider-Man watched as the last of the residents was led out of the building. "That's it!" called the fire chief. "Everyone's safe!"

That's when a woman came running up to the firefighters. "My baby! My baby!" she wailed. "She's still inside!"

"There's a baby inside!" one of the firefighters shouted, strapping an oxygen tank to his back. Spider-Man ran forward. The man's smoke-blackened face looked exhausted. "I know this is your job," Spider-Man said, "but let me, please."

The woman told Spider-Man which window

was the baby's room, so he shot his web at the nearest fire escape. But the web melted! The fire was so incredibly hot! Spider-Man quickly shot another web at the building across the street and swung across as fast as he could. *Crash!* He broke the window with his feet and landed with a thump in the dark apartment.

The smoke was so thick that Spider-Man could hardly see. Where was the baby? Was she okay? He concentrated as hard as he could with his spider sense—and could just make out a faint crying in the corner of the room. He followed along in the dark, and bumped into the baby's crib! He carefully bundled her in a blanket, dove out the window, and swung them both to safety.

The crowd cheered, and the look on the mother's face when Peter handed over her baby was something he would never forget for the rest of his life. "Thank you, Spider-Man," she said. "You saved my baby."

Peter collected his camera gear, put his clothes back on, and headed to work. He was

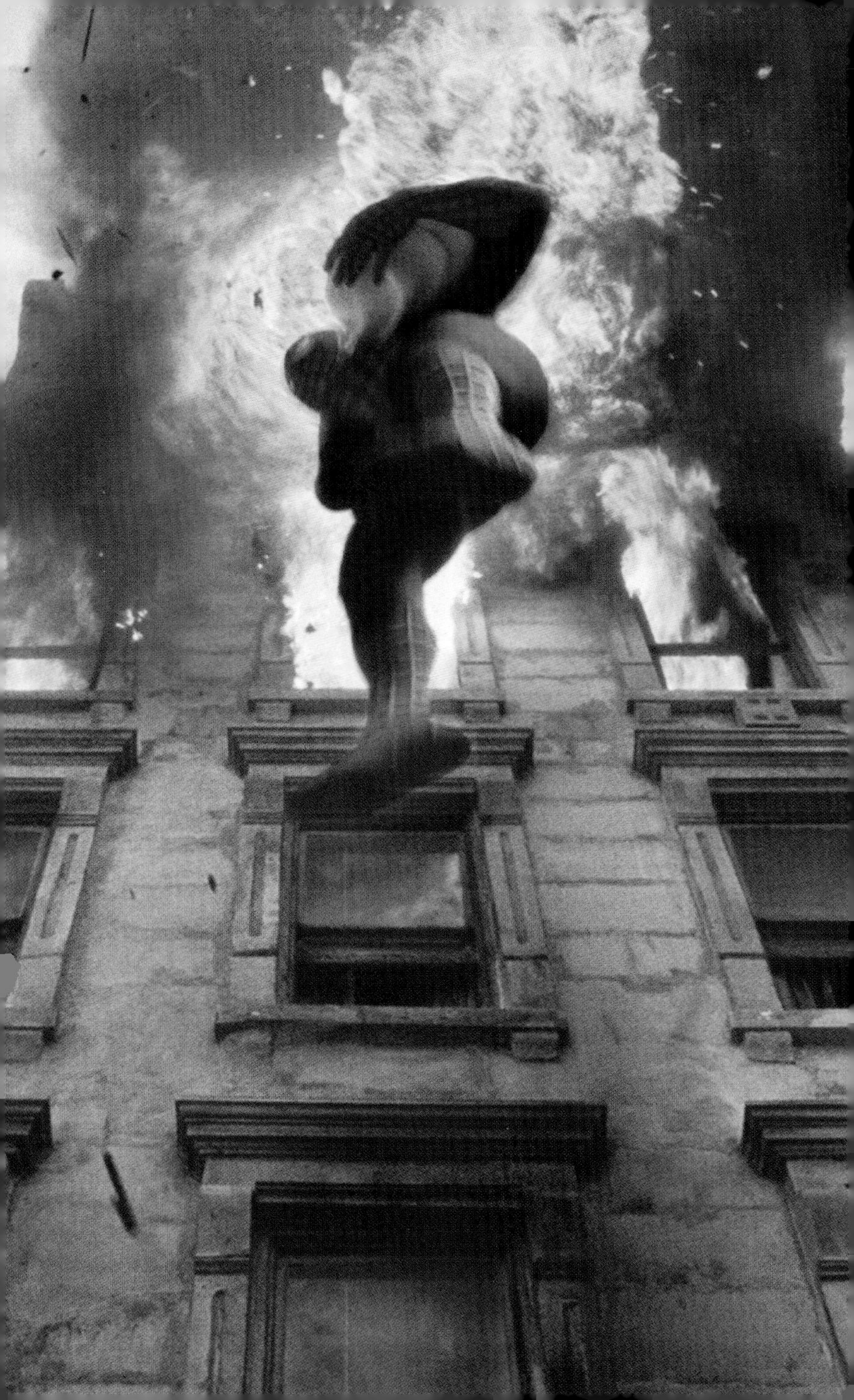

late. Hopefully J. Jonah Jameson wouldn't notice . . .

"Parker, you're late!" Jonah bellowed. He sniffed the air. "And not only that—you stink! I hope you have a good excuse!"

"The best, Boss," said Peter with a smile. "Hope you've got some space on page one for what I've got in this camera!"

And Jonah did something he very rarely did—he smiled a very big smile.

New York's Favorite Newspaper Since 1932

DAILY BUGLE

www.dailybugle.com   50¢

SPIDER-MAN'S HOT AS BLAZES

By Tony Targo.

Spider-Man became an official member of New York's Bravest this morning as he swung into a burning building to rescue a baby. "It was inspiring," said Fire Chief George Bailey. "All New York City Firefighters take their helmets off to Spider-Man for his selfless act

(continued on page 4)

CHAPTER 6

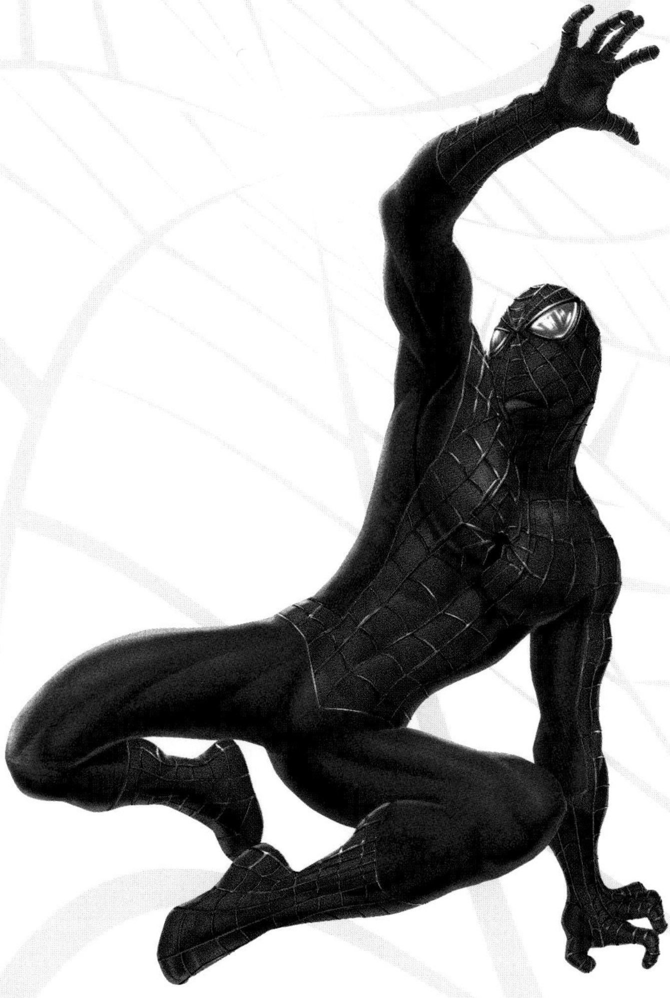

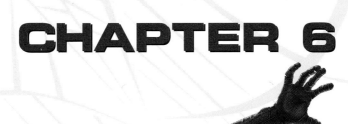

SPIDER-MAN

HOLDUP!

"**M**mmm! Smells great!" said Peter as he walked into Aunt May's house. She had invited Peter and a couple of her neighbors over for Sunday supper. She was making Peter's favorite—meatloaf, mashed potatoes, and green beans, with coconut cream pie for dessert. Peter's stomach rumbled in anticipation.

"So how was your day today?" Aunt May asked. "Is that Jameson fellow being any nicer to you?"

Peter shrugged. He sat at the kitchen table and was just about to stick his finger into the steaming-hot potatoes for a taste. "Hold it right there, young man!" Aunt May

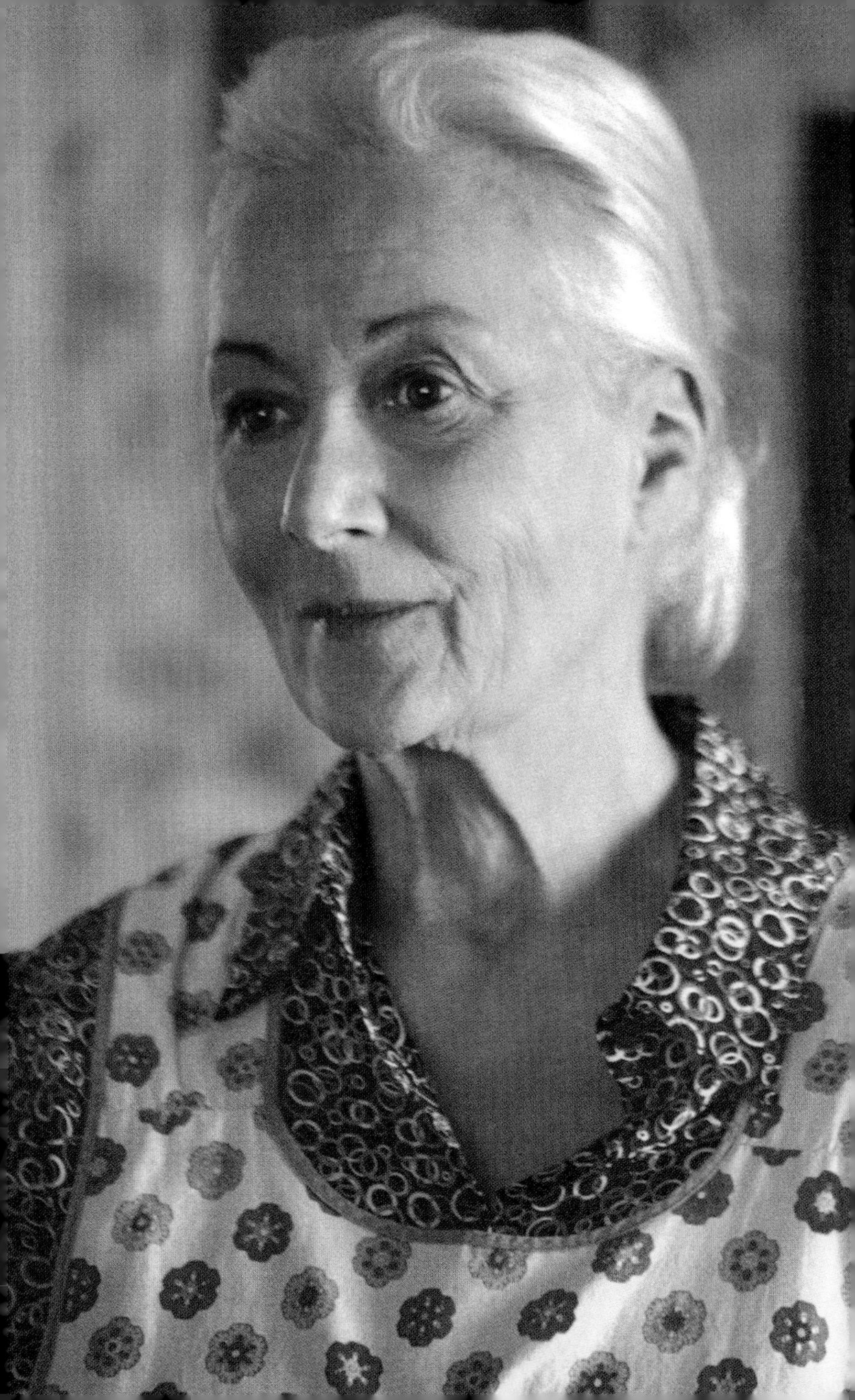

said with a laugh as she playfully slapped his hand. "They're not done yet!" she scolded. She opened the refrigerator and looked around. "Oh, dear," she said. "I'm out of butter!" She began to untie her apron. "I'll just run down to the Lees' and . . ."

Peter jumped up. "Don't be silly, Aunt May. You stay here and finish up everything else, and I'll run to the store."

"Thank you, dear," said Aunt May, putting her hand to his cheek. "Hurry back. The neighbors will be here soon."

Peter put on his jacket and made his way down the block and around the corner to the grocery store. He'd been buying baseball cards and gumballs from the Lees for as long as he could remember. He hadn't paid a visit to the neighborhood in a while and he knew it would be good to see them.

As he rounded the corner, a thuggish-looking guy in a black leather coat and dark sunglasses slammed right into him. "Pardon me," Peter said. Aunt May had always taught him to be polite. The guy just kept going.

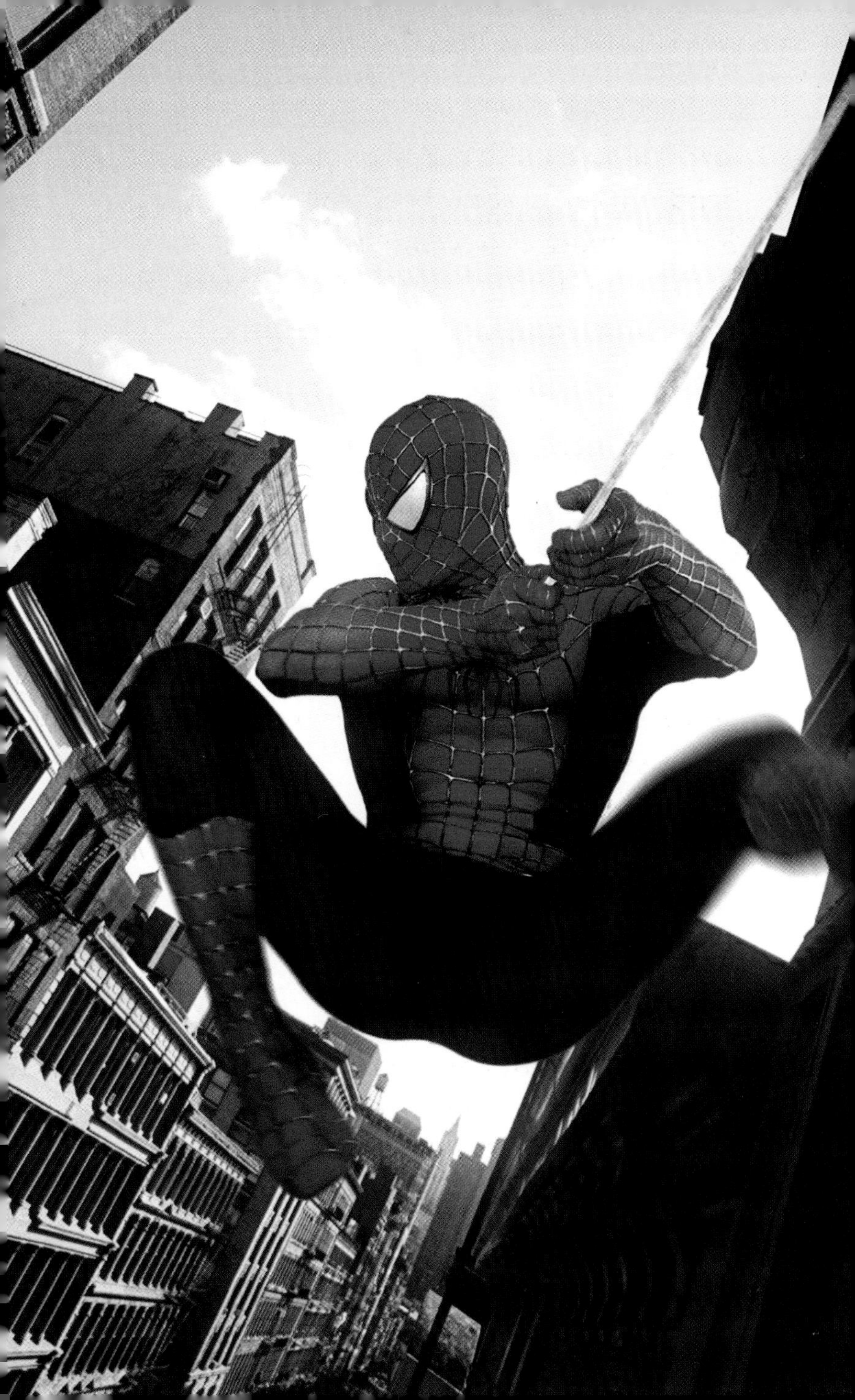

Peter was just about to open the grocery store's door when it burst open and Mr. Lee came running out. "Stop! Thief!" he cried.

"Black coat and sunglasses?" Peter asked.

"Yes!" shouted Mr. Lee. "He got all our money!"

Peter ran down the block. But where did the thief go?

Peter quickly turned down an alley between two buildings. Moments after changing into his Spider-Man costume, he was scaling the side of a building. He swung from rooftop to rooftop, searching.

There! The guy was standing right below him, stuffing his pockets with the Lees' money!

Quietly, Spider-Man descended along the side of the building. He was just about to make his move when the guy suddenly spun around and pulled out a gun. He pointed it right at Spider-Man.

"Back off," the guy growled.

"Give me back that money. It doesn't belong to you!" Spider-Man shouted angrily.

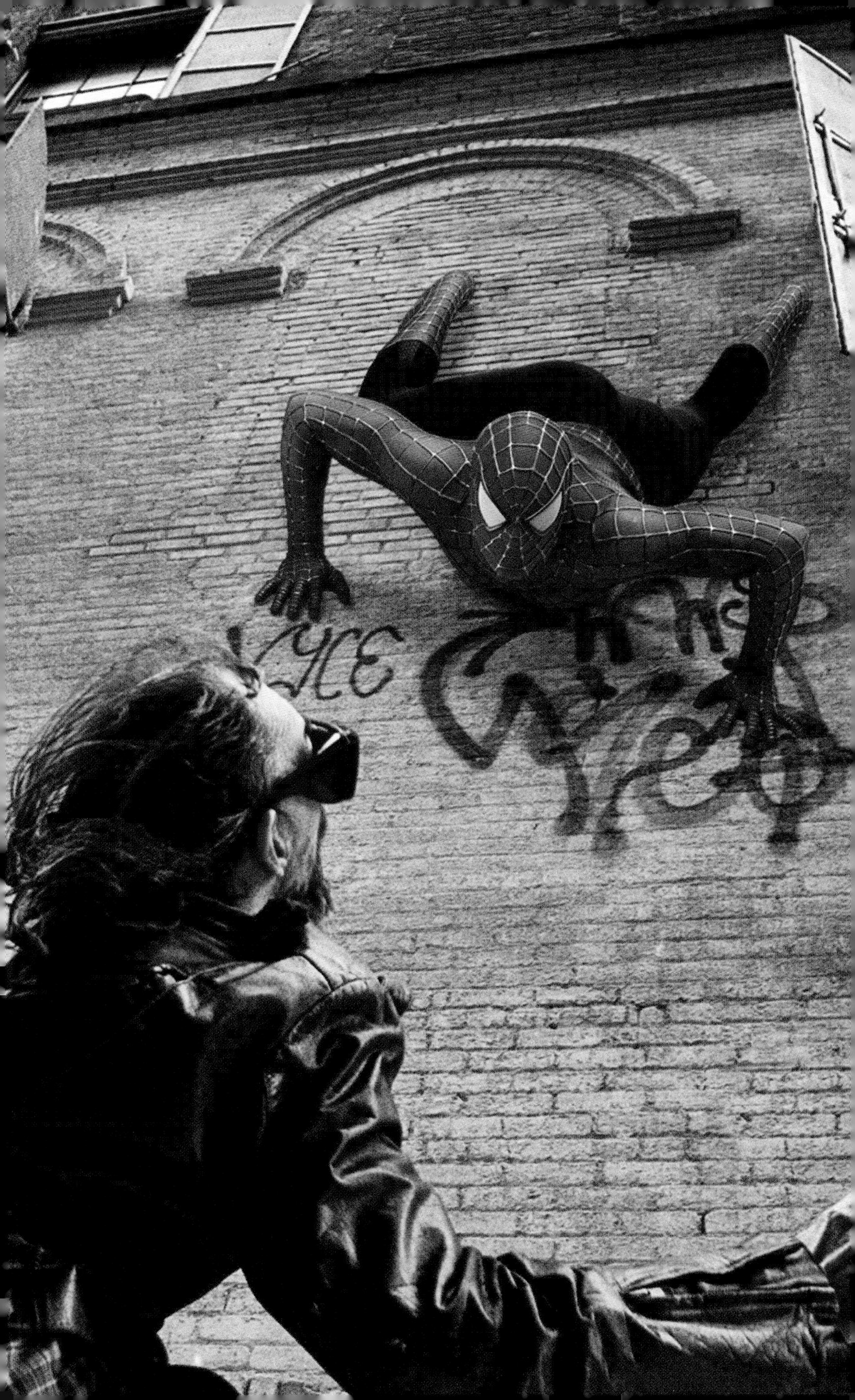

"Well, it's mine now," the guy said with a sneer, backing away down the alley, his gun trained on Spider-Man. "Don't move a muscle and I won't shoot," he said.

Spider-Man knew what he had to do and he knew he had to be fast—faster than he'd ever been before. With one lightning-quick motion he twisted his wrist and aimed his webbing right at the gun. In that split second, the robber squeezed the trigger. But he wasn't fast enough. The gun was jerked out of his hand at the same moment that it went off, and the bullet harmlessly ricocheted off a building. The thief stared in disbelief at his empty hand, then took off running down the alley. Spidey dropped to the ground, flipped through the air over the guy, and landed at the end of the alley. Quickly he spun a huge web across the entrance and stood back. The robber ran right into the web and stuck there fast! Just then the police arrived to make their arrest.

* * *

When Peter arrived home, all the neighbors were sitting around the table, looking impatient.

"Catching up with the Lees?" asked the neighbor from across the street, Mr. Walsh.

"Where's the butter, Peter?" Aunt May asked gently.

Peter gave everyone an apologetic smile and raced back outside.

On his way out Peter could hear Mrs. Bergen from down the block laugh. "That boy would forget his head if it wasn't attached to his shoulders!" she said.

New York's Favorite Newspaper Since 1932

DAILY

An exclusive interview with Tony Targo

He's saved babies from burning buildings, defeated dangerous criminals, saved banks from being robbed and saved small-business owners from stick-up men. He keeps our neighborhoods safe and sound.

But it's all in a day's work for Spider-Man. The webslinger is not one to rest on his laurels, or brag of his accomplishments.

"Why do you do the things you do?" this reporter asked him. "Why do you risk your life to save others?"

Spider-Man thought for a moment. "A wise man once told me that with great power comes great responsibility." He paused. "I've always lived by those words."

But when asked who uttered these words, Spider-Man seemed too choked up to answer.

"Oops!" said the webslinger. "I've got to run. My spider sense is tingling again!"

As Spider-Man turned to leave he offered an important piece of advice.

"Remember, if you need help I am never far away. Just call me, your friendly neighborhood Spider-Man!"

Thanking this reporter for his time, Spider-Man swung right out the window. Who would he be saving this time? Your guess is as good as mine. Whatever he left to do, we can only assume that it was good and brave and heroic.

Good luck, Spider-Man. And thank you.

NOTE: The *Daily Bugle* regrets that we had to run an existing photo of Spider-Man with this story, but our freelance photographer arrived right after Spider-Man left the scene, missing the superhero by seconds.

BUGLE

www.dailybugle.com 50¢

OUR FRIENDLY NEIGHBORHOOD SPIDER-MAN

PETER PARKER'S TOP TEN SUPER SPIDER-POWERS:

1 Ability to shoot spiderwebbing out of his wrists by flipping hand over and bending middle and index fingers.

2 Ability to scale buildings with special spider-adhesive action.

3 Ability to spin webs strong enough to stop criminals in their tracks.

4 Keen eyesight for spotting foul play.

5 Spider sense—which warns him when something bad is about to happen.

6 A huge spider-appetite.

7 Lightning-quick reflexes.

8 Amazing spider-strength.

9 Acrobatic moves of a trained gymnast.

10 And Peter's personal favorite—he can hang upside down from the ceiling! Great for surprise attacks on bad guys. (It's kind of like what that laboratory spider did to him!)